GOOD DOG, McTAVISH

Meg Rosoff

ILLUSTRATED BY **GRACE EASTON**

CANDLEWICK PRESS

First published by Barrington Stoke, Ltd. (Great Britain), 2017
First US paperback edition 2022

Library of Congress Catalog Card Number 2018961319
ISBN 978-1-5362-0058-4 (hardcover)
ISBN 978-1-5362-2603-4 (paperback)

22 23 24 25 26 27 TRC 10 9 8 7 6 5 4 3 2 1

Printed in Eagan, MN, USA

This book was typeset in Lora.
The illustrations were done in mixed media and collage.

Candlewick Press
99 Dover Street
Somerville, Massachusetts 02144

www.candlewick.com

To the real McTavish,
illustrious rogue and rascal

CONTENTS

1
McTavish Falls
for the Peacheys

McTavish's decision to adopt the Peachey family was not the most sensible decision of his life. He could tell at once that they were not one of those easy families, the ones that fit effortlessly into a dog's life. He could tell that they were a family with problems.

Whether they'd been traumatized early on or were just difficult by nature, McTavish had no way of knowing. But he did know that adopting them would require patience, discipline, and hard work. His logical mind told him to wait for a trouble-free family, a family with easy natures and cheerful smiles. But there was something about the Peacheys, with their sad little faces, that clinched it for him.

Oh, McTavish, he warned himself. Are you sure you're not making a mistake? Beware! This could mean years of heartache and frustration.

But it was already too late.

McTavish had fallen for the Peacheys.

2
MA PEACHEY GIVES UP

McTavish might never have met the Peacheys if Ma Peachey hadn't decided to give up being a mother.

"I give up," she said. "No more cooking and cleaning and finding lost keys. No more keeping track of your appointments and nagging you to clean up your rooms. No more boring, thankless jobs. I quit."

At first, the younger Peacheys rejoiced.

"No more healthy food!" shouted Ollie, age twelve, punching the air in triumph.

"No more matriarchal oppression!" crowed Ava, age fourteen, looking up from the book she was reading (*The Family: A History of Despair*).

No more nagging to get home in time for dinner, thought Pa Peachey, though of course he would never have said such a thing out loud.

The youngest member of the family frowned.

"Ma," said Betty Peachey, age eight, "are you saying that you've . . . resigned?"

Ma Peachey smiled. "Why, yes, Betty. That's an excellent way of putting it."

Betty looked concerned. "Is that legal?"

Ma Peachey shrugged. "Maybe it is,

maybe it isn't. But I'm sick and tired of everyone making a mess and expecting me to clean it up. I'm done with cooking meals that get cold because no one's home to eat them. And," she said, "I'm tired of having to shout at everyone to wake up, go to bed, put away the laundry, say please, say thank you, clear the dishes, stop fighting."

"But –" Betty began.

Ma Peachey ignored her. "So yes," she said, "you could say I've resigned. For now, anyway. I am taking time out to pursue peace and quiet. From now on, the only person I am in charge of is me."

And with that, she gave Betty a kiss on the head, and went off to change into her yoga pants.

At first, none of the Peacheys really missed being told to clear the table or put

away the laundry. But as days turned to weeks and nobody made dinner or washed the clothes – ever – the sense of freedom wore thin.

The Peacheys ate frozen dinners or take-out every night, wore the same clothes over and over, and arrived late to school and work each day. There was a great deal more squabbling and a great deal more squalor.

Betty, who was by far the most sensible member of the Peachey family (after Ma Peachey), began to feel that some sort of intervention was required. And so, one Saturday afternoon just before Easter, a family conference was held.

"Due to the loss of motherly care in our family, I am feeling lost, lonesome, and lacking in love," said Betty.

Ava and Ollie snickered, but Betty ignored them.

"I have a proposal," she said.

The rest of the Peacheys leaned forward expectantly. Across the room, Ma Peachey hummed as she worked on her lotus position.

"We could ask Ma Peachey to come back," said Betty.

Ava gasped, Ollie snorted, and Pa Peachey made a tut-tut noise, one that did not commit him to any opinion but that still managed to express disapproval.

Silence fell.

"Well," said Betty at last, "if we are not planning to ask Ma Peachey to come back, I have another suggestion."

Once again, the Peacheys all leaned forward to listen.

"I believe we should get a dog."

Ollie imagined a big, handsome, furry creature that might help him be more attractive to girls.

Ava imagined a large, melancholy dog that would help her look more intellectual.

Pa Peachey did not want a dog. At all. And he said so.

A heated discussion ensued, and, in the end, the three Peachey children managed to prevail. They would take a trip to the animal shelter.

"Not to adopt a dog," Pa Peachey warned. "Just to browse."

"To browse?" Ollie rolled his eyes. "We're going to *browse* lonely stray dogs doomed to spend eternity locked up, sad and loveless, in cages?" He turned to Ava and lowered his voice to a stage whisper. "I always said there was something heartless about Pa Peachey."

Ava scowled. "Nobody browses homeless dogs. Except perhaps" – she turned to glare at her father – "a sociopath."

"Never mind," said Betty. "We shall go to the shelter to browse, and perhaps, just perhaps, we shall find the dog of our dreams."

Ollie rolled his eyes.

Ava carefully recorded this conversation in a brown notebook. She had hopes that her book, *Memoir of a Broken Childhood*, would sell for a large sum of money and become an international bestseller.

Ollie went back to the book he was reading, feeling (perhaps correctly) that the last thing the world needed was another book, particularly one written by his older sister.

3

BROWSING

The following afternoon, the Peachey family (minus Ma Peachey, who was working on her warrior pose) assembled at exactly two o'clock and set off in Pa Peachey's van, which was so full of screws and springs and gizmos and stuff-that-might-someday-come-in-handy that there was barely any place for an actual human to sit.

Ava complained about the noise the van

made, but no one else seemed to hear, partly because it was so noisy in the van.

Pa Peachey pulled up in front of the Cuddles Home for Unclaimed Mutts (C.H.U.M.) with a little flourish and a spin of the steering wheel.

He set the parking brake with a loud squeak and shouted "OUT, OUT, OUT" over his shoulder, as if the children had been sitting in the parked van for months.

All the Peachey children were excited by the possibility that they might soon acquire a dog – even Ava, who was famous for being hard as nails and sentimental as burnt wood.

"I can't wait to browse the poor homeless doggies," Ava whispered to Ollie.

Ollie imagined the future Peachey family dog, waiting on the other side of that door, locked in a lonely cage. The thought made him feel quite light-headed.

Betty screwed her eyes shut with longing and terror. She did not want to browse dogs. All she wanted was to choose the smartest, waggliest, most shiny-eyed of all the poor doggies in captivity, take him home, and love him to bits. Maybe then the family could return to a time when Ma Peachey wasn't doing yoga, Pa Peachey wasn't angry, and Ava, Ollie, and Betty didn't feel quite so much like orphans.

Inside the shelter, McTavish waited quietly, not barking, not making a fuss. Just . . . waiting. Although he hadn't met the Peacheys, he had a dog's sixth sense about this family. He had a feeling they might be "the one."

Pa Peachey went in first, followed by Ollie, Ava, and Betty.

Betty was always last. Last was what happened when your parents decided to stop having children once you were born. There was no one less important to tease, annoy, and torment.

Inside the Cuddles Home for Unclaimed Mutts, a stern-looking woman in overalls greeted the Peacheys. Her name tag read *Hello. I'm Ian.*

"Hello, I'm Alice," she said.

"Not Ian?" Ava was a stickler for accuracy in the written word.

Alice/Ian looked confused for a second, then followed the direction of eight eyes and bent her head to peer at the name tag with a sigh.

"The overalls may say Ian, but please look beyond that. I am not Ian. I am Alice." She paused to scan the family with a practiced eye.

The family scanned her back.

"You are here for a dog," Alice announced, as if the thought had not occurred to the Peacheys. As if perhaps they had just stumbled into the Cuddles Home for Unclaimed Mutts on a shopping trip, thinking it might be a good place to buy a newspaper and a carton of milk.

"Yes, we are," Betty piped up.

"No, we are most certainly *not* here for a dog," Pa Peachey said with a glare at his youngest child. "We are here to determine the lay of the land. We are not in the market for a canine at this moment in time. We are here to undertake an initial foray into the acquisition of a family pet. At some future date. Going forward."

Ollie made crazy motions with one finger in the air by his left ear, and Ava turned her hands into quacking ducks.

"We are here," Betty said in a soft and clear voice, "for a dog."

Despite all the time she spent complaining about being the youngest, Betty often forgot to notice that she held a position of great authority in the Peachey family.

Alice held up her hand. "I am getting a picture of this family," she said, looking down her rather long nose and out through her rather thick glasses. "I am getting the picture of a family that is not always in harmony with its desires. Is that what you would call an accurate picture of your family?"

"Yes," said Betty.

"No," said Pa Peachey.

"Sometimes," said Ava.

"Rarely," said Ollie.

Betty sighed. "*They* are all confused. But I am not. I am here. For a dog."

From that moment on, Alice addressed all her remarks to Betty. Who was, it is probably worth restating, not yet nine years old.

"Good," said Alice. "Because we have too many dogs and not enough humans to take them home and love them. Now, please sit."

Obediently, the Peachey family sat.

4
ALICE'S
QUESTIONS

"Now," said Alice. "I am going to ask you
some questions, and I'd be grateful if only
one of you answered at a time. You," she said,
indicating Betty. "You seem to be the least
lunatic member of the family, so I would like
you to answer my questions. If any other
person objects, please raise your paw." She
paused. "I mean hand."

The Peacheys nodded.

"Excellent. Question one. Does your home have a fenced yard?"

"Yes," said Betty. "Our home has a fenced yard with one apple tree, uncut grass due to arguments about whose turn it is to cut it, and many, many squirrels for a woofy love-dog to chase."

Alice checked off box one.

"Question two. How much exercise does a dog need each day?"

Betty thought for a moment. "I would take my dog for a walk before school each morning, and Pa Peachey would walk him again at night. Ava and Ollie could take turns walking him after school."

Alice tapped her pencil on the desk and nodded. "Question three. What are the four most important things in a dog's life? You may all confer."

They conferred, ignoring one another entirely.

"Food," said Pa Peachey.

"Water," said Ollie, who had recently learned in biology that you could go weeks without food but only a few days without water.

"A sense of philosophical autonomy," said Ava, who always went for the existential option. Which nobody understood.

When they were done, Betty turned to Alice with quiet dignity. "The most important thing for any dog is love. After that, it's routine. Then exercise and mental stimulation and – last of all – healthy food."

"Thank you, Betty," Alice said. "You are

very wise for a young person. Particularly for a young person who has obviously been raised by wolves." She gazed sternly at Pa Peachey.

"And of course a comfy bed," Betty added. "And not being dressed up in silly clothes, like snow boots. Or little raincoats."

"All good answers. And finally, I must ask each of you if you understand the commitment dog ownership entails."

"A painfully long one," said Pa Peachey in a mournful voice.

"It's like having another sibling," said Ava. "That bites."

"It can't be worse than a younger sister," grumbled Ollie.

Betty looked at each member of the family in turn. "I imagine that it is halfway between having a friend and a baby," she said after a moment. "A dog requires a great deal of attention and care but can also be a fine companion. A dog will love you and make you feel happy when you are lonely or low, in exchange for a life of order and kindness."

Alice jotted down some more notes. She looked up at last.

"One of you gets it," she said, tapping her pencil against the table. "And that may well be enough. I shall have to think about it. But for now, let us go and meet the dogs."

She stood and led the way to the kennels at the back. A great barking and whining started up.

"Oh my," Pa Peachey said, turning pale.

The Peachey family began to browse.

There were hairy dogs and smooth dogs, huge dogs and tiny dogs, lolling drooling dogs and neat-footed dogs as tidy as cats.

Some had stripy brown coats, others were black and white, and one was a lovely, fluffy, lemony sort of color.

Ollie fell in love with a huge spotted beast that looked like a Dalmatian crossed with a dinosaur.

Pa Peachey cast admiring glances at a loyal Labrador with big amber eyes.

Ava made cooing noises at a nervous little thing that looked like a wolfhound shrunk in the wash.

Betty walked from cage to cage, her eyes sometimes filling with tears, her fists balled with determination.

After nearly an hour of watching the Peachey family browse dogs, Alice looked down and found Betty standing by her side.

"I would like to adopt every single one of these lovely doggingtons," Betty said. "But I believe I have found the one special dog for us." She took Alice's hand and led her to a quiet crate near the corner.

"Him," Betty said, pointing.

Alice peered at the name on the crate. She looked inside, just to make 100 percent sure.

"McTavish," she said at last, and she smiled a small smile.

"Is that his name?" Betty asked.

Alice nodded.

Betty tilted her head and frowned. "What exactly is . . . McTavish?"

"Well," said Alice, "he is quite a lot of Scottish terrier, a bit of Jack Russell, a touch of poodle, a trace of Tibetan spaniel . . . and perhaps just a dash of" – she leaned in close to Betty, raised one eyebrow, lowered her voice, and whispered – "*Bichon Frisé.*"

Betty giggled. "McTavish," she said, and knelt down to his level. The dog and the child looked into each other's eyes for a long moment. A very long moment.

Betty spoke at last. "I think I would like you to come home with us," she said to McTavish in a polite voice. "That is, if you think you might like us."

McTavish looked at Betty and cocked his head to one side, thinking.

After what seemed like a very long time, he took one step forward, stuck his nose through the bars of the crate, and swiped Betty's face with his tongue.

Alice opened the door to the cage, put a leash on McTavish, and led him through to the Getting to Know You room. She sent Betty to collect the rest of the Peachey family.

"He's a bit short," Ollie said.

"Is it morally appropriate for one species to own another species?" Ava wondered aloud.

"McTavish?" Pa Peachey asked, looking worried. "Is he a foreign dog?"

Betty ignored them all. "He is a perfect dog," she said. "He is beautiful and intelligent and sensible. We will love and cherish McTavish, and he will become an important and admired member of our family."

Alice took pictures on her phone, so the Peacheys would remember their first visit with the newest member of their family. The pictures showed a dog quite a bit longer than he was high, with huge triangular ears that stood up like a bat's. He had soft brown eyes, a thoughtful expression, large paws, and a wiry golden coat that stuck out in all directions.

"His first owner was an elderly lady who became ill and could no longer care for him," Alice told them. "So he has not had a bad start in life. He is four years old, and he knows his own mind. There is no question that he would make an excellent dog for this family. My question," she said, and she narrowed her eyes a little, "is whether you will make a good family for this dog."

"A dog is for life, not just for Easter," Pa Peachey warned, but no one took any notice.

McTavish looked at Betty with a serious expression. And then he bobbed his head, took a neat step into her lap, lay down, and sighed.

"McTavish has spoken," said Alice.

5

GETTING READY FOR MCTAVISH

Certain matters needed to be settled before McTavish took up residence with the Peacheys. Alice made a visit to the Peachey home.

"She wants to check that we're not a front for international dog smugglers," Ava said.

Ollie looked up from his book. "Is that even a thing?"

Ava shrugged. "Everything's a thing."

"We are not a front for international dog

smugglers," Ollie said to Alice. "In case you were wondering."

"I wasn't," said Alice, and handed Betty an information folder with a list of everything they would need for the safety and happiness of their new dog. "Now, where are you planning to put his bed?" she asked.

"He will sleep with me," Betty said.

"No, he will not," Alice said in a very stern voice. "A dog needs his own bed in a warm and quiet place." She looked around and settled on a snug corner under the stairs. "This corner will do perfectly. McTavish will have privacy and as much peace and quiet as he needs. He will be able to keep an eye on the comings and goings of every person in this somewhat peculiar household."

And that was that.

Alice approved the Peacheys' application

to re-home McTavish and arranged to return the following morning with McTavish himself. She said she would also bring a collar and leash and a week's worth of food.

Just then, Pa Peachey emerged from his study and snatched the information folder from Betty's hand.

"A shopping list?" he exclaimed. "A shopping list for a dog? Whatever next? Ballet lessons? Summer camp?"

Betty opened her mouth to explain, but Pa Peachey waved for silence.

"A bed," he exclaimed. "A bed for a dog? What nonsense. Why not a dog automobile? Or a dog airplane? Any animal worth his salt would make his own bed. He'd burrow down under the house, carry in straw and moss, and live there in a nest. That's what dogs did in my day."

The three children stared at him blankly.

"In your day," Ollie said, "dinosaurs roamed the earth."

Pa Peachey ignored him. "And what's this? Dog food? He's a predator, for Pete's sake. Send the lazy so-and-so out to hunt for his own food."

Betty stepped forward. "Pa," she said, "McTavish is not a predator. He is a house dog, a companion and friend. A domestic animal. He would require years of training to learn to fend for himself. He might even take to preying upon cats or small children. Which would soon present other problems."

Betty had a good way of dealing with Pa Peachey that the two older children admired greatly.

"Pfft," Pa Peachey said, which was his way of backing down. "What else am I being fleeced for?" He scanned the list and handed it back to Betty. "This whole dog nonsense is nothing but a, a, a . . ." Unable to think of an appropriate word to end the sentence, he left the room.

Betty disappeared into the attic and returned with a grubby flannel sleeping bag left over from Ava's Girl Scout days and an old gray wool blanket. She stuffed the sleeping bag and the blanket into the washing machine and turned it on. When both were clean and dry, she sat down in front of the TV with a large needle and a ball of red yarn from her mother's knitting basket. With a pair of scissors, she trimmed the blanket into one large rectangle. Then, with big red stitches, she began to sew the edges together while watching a documentary about the intelligence of starfish.

"Hello, dear," Ma Peachey said as she passed through the house on her way to her evening yoga class.

"Hello, Ma," said Betty. "We have adopted a dog. His name is McTavish, and I think you will like him."

"How nice," said Ma Peachey. "But who is planning to walk and feed and care for McTavish?"

"We are," said Betty, and returned to her sewing.

Ma Peachey picked up her yoga bag and smiled a small smile.

"Excellent," she said to no one in particular.

Once Betty had sewn the blanket into a pocket, she stuffed the sleeping bag inside, punched it around, sewed up the open side, and settled the warm and fluffy new bed into the corner under the stairs.

"There," she said with satisfaction. "McTavish doggity-dog will love this."

And how could he not? It was cozy and squishy and clean, it was gray wool with a bold red blanket stitch around the edges, and even Ava was tempted to sneak into the corner and settle down for a little read.

But she didn't. Because Betty would have squawked.

6

McTavish
Comes Home

McTavish made himself at home at once.

He discovered his new bed, stamped it down, and dug around with his paws until the sleeping bag stuffing shifted to his exact specifications. Then he turned around four times and settled with his rump toward the corner and his head pointed out at the rest of the house.

As Alice had predicted, it was a good spot. It allowed McTavish to monitor who

was upstairs and who was down, who was coming in the front door and who was going out the back. He could see who was skulking in the kitchen looking for leftovers – and who was prowling aimlessly, seeking a fight.

That person was nearly always Pa Peachey.

Pa Peachey had not been happy of late.

Although not a cheerful baby and quite a pessimistic child, Pa Peachey's bad temper took a serious turn when Ma Peachey announced her latest plan.

"I am going to India to explore my spiritual self. With my new yoga teacher, Wyatt," she said.

Pa Peachey frowned. Wyatt was a very handsome young man, with flexible shoulders, firm thighs, and a serene expression.

Ollie, Ava, and Betty thought Wyatt looked very calm and could understand why Ma Peachey found him restful after so many years with Pa Peachey.

Pa Peachey may have been gloomy, but he was a passionate man. He felt passionate about most subjects, including family, the history of the lawn mower, and whether or not to get a dog. So when Ma Peachey said she was going away with Wyatt, the serene and handsome yoga teacher, he went a bit – well, there's no other word for it: he went a bit loopy.

He shouted. He stomped around. He criticized the children and tried to kick the dog.

While Pa Peachey went loopy, Ma Peachey practiced yoga. Ollie, Ava, and Betty tried to stay out of sight. Chaos reigned in the Peachey household. Chaos, that is, in the form of arguments, bad temper, and a general mood of gloom.

This was how McTavish found things when he first arrived at his new home. He observed the Peacheys in silence, needing to know what sort of family he had chosen, and what his role in that family would be.

In case you are still not certain, McTavish was not one of those ball-chasing, hole-digging dogs you meet so often in books. McTavish was more of a psychological mastermind. He liked to organize people, to fix situations that were not to his liking. And to arrange the world in a way that made it most comfortable for himself.

McTavish felt a strong bond with the

younger Peacheys (particularly, of course, with Betty), but he had some very definite concerns about the older Peacheys.

All that first day, he lay on his bed, not barking to go out, not begging for food or asking to play ball. Instead, he observed.

Here is what he observed.

He observed that Pa Peachey was not a bad person, but that he had a cranky, resentful side.

He observed that Ma Peachey had turned to yoga to escape from her family, and that she would almost certainly return someday. But perhaps one reason she needed to escape was that she had become fed up with Pa Peachey's cranky, resentful side.

McTavish also observed that despite the Peachey children's niceness, intelligence, and good manners, they had many failings.

For instance, they failed to pick up after themselves, and they failed to take much notice of anyone else in the family.

McTavish observed that the one member of the family without any great failings was Betty. He observed Betty with a strange sort of pride. Betty was, after all, his main person in the family. And a most superior sort of person she was, for a human.

However, even an ordinary, run-of-the-mill dog (and McTavish was no ordinary dog) could see that the Peachey family had a problem. And it was clear that the family problem needed to be solved if McTavish was to get any peace and quiet.

So he set to work.

7

THE PEACHEY PROBLEM

"Where are the keys?" Pa Peachey thundered.

"Who's stolen my homework?" Ava Peachey shouted.

"We're out of milk," Ollie Peachey moaned.

It was nine a.m., and nearly every member of the Peachey family was late. Late for breakfast, late for school, just plain late.

In addition, the Peachey kitchen was

so cluttered with papers and books and discarded items of clothing that it was impossible to navigate from table to fridge, much less to prepare meals there. Breakfast was a disaster, lunch was impossible, and dinner barely deserved a mention.

Pa Peachey had taken to buying microwave meals that required no pans and almost no cleaning up. Which was a success. Except that none of the Peacheys actually liked microwave meals.

Ma Peachey was too busy meditating to care what the family ate for dinner. She lived on brown rice and clean thoughts.

"These meals are really very convenient," Pa Peachey said. He did not dwell on the fact that they tasted horrible. They were full of sugar and salt and chemicals that made your head feel bad and your wallet feel empty.

Not to mention all the plastic, foil, and guilt about destruction of the rain forest.

McTavish began to wonder if anyone in the Peachey family even knew how to cook. It wasn't so much that he hated the dry food Alice had brought from the shelter, but he would have much preferred a nice lamb bone now and again with some leftover vegetables and bacon rind.

Or at the very least, a tasty spinach-and-goat-cheese omelet.

"Where are my keys?" Pa Peachey shouted for the twelfth time that morning. "No one will get to school if I can't find my keys."

"I don't care about your keys," Ava wailed. "Why is there no clean underwear? I'm going to be late *again*."

"*Ohmmmmm*," Ma Peachey chanted, on her way to inner peace.

It was obvious why no one could find anything.

The clean and dirty laundry sat together in a tangled mess on a large armchair formerly used for sitting. Shoes (never in pairs) seemed to stray around the house at random, turning up in the most unexpected places – the back seat of the car, the bottom drawer of Pa Peachey's desk, the broom closet. Keys wandered out of pockets and disappeared forever.

The Peachey household was a mess.

McTavish laid his head on his front paws and gazed at the ceiling. He knew that humans were an inferior race, but their foolishness never ceased to amaze him.

Why? he thought. *Why can't they think for themselves?*

Any dog worth his salt could organize his

way into a family. The key was to arrange regular meals and walks and concentrate on snoozing most of the day while the humans did all the work and earned the money to pay for all of it. Really clever dogs also sometimes got pigs' ears and trips to the country, and no one made them pay for gas or the B&B.

In contrast, moderately clever humans worked at jobs they hated with bosses they couldn't stand, slaving long hours and becoming more and more unhappy. Once or twice a year, they went away for a week to the beach, where it always rained.

Sometimes McTavish felt a little sorry for humans. There was no question at all that even a run-of-the-mill dog had a better life than a moderately clever human, though every human McTavish had ever met considered himself vastly superior to all other members of the animal kingdom.

Humans were puzzlingly dim.

McTavish sighed. There was so much work to do.

PLAN A

Betty was at the end of her rope.

She hated seeing her father unhappy. She hated microwave dinners. She hated all the mess in the house. She hated the fact that everyone overslept and was late for school. And she hated the fact that her mother had changed – from a fairly ordinary mother with a proper job, who cooked and cleaned and got everyone out of bed and to school at the right time, to the opposite of all that.

Betty's mother had quite an important job as an accountant. These days, she still went to work, but she spent all her spare time meditating, perfecting the lotus in tripod position or her handstand scorpion. And planning her trip to India.

A mother might want to abandon her family to seek inner peace, Betty thought, *but it's not very nice for the family.*

Mothers were meant to dedicate themselves to keeping order and good cheer, while having their own careers and reminding the father of the house which child's birthday was next week and when the dishwasher needed unloading.

Weren't they?

Betty thought a great deal about this subject.

What is the purpose of a mother? she wondered.

The fact that family life was going downhill since Ma Peachey had stopped making it her first priority suggested that mothers held some sort of key to family happiness. Yes, fathers were important, but mothers were fundamental.

Now, Betty may have been not quite nine years old, but she considered herself a feminist. She did not like the idea that the Peacheys were incapable of preparing decent meals and keeping the house clean while Ma Peachey sought inner peace.

Surely they could exist in the absence of a full-time mother?

Betty discussed the situation with McTavish. She and McTavish went on long walks together. They sat on McTavish's bed and talked – or at least Betty talked, while McTavish listened. Betty and McTavish had remarkably similar temperaments given that they came from completely different species. They both required harmony and order. And so, they became allies.

Now, if you think that dogs mostly dream of juicy bones and comfy beds, I can tell you that this is not true. McTavish spent a great deal of his time coming up with plans. After only a few days with the Peacheys, and after consulting with Betty, a really excellent plan began to form in his head.

He called it Plan A.

The first element of Plan A required

McTavish to collect all the discarded sweaters and blankets and socks and pillows in the house, and drag them into his corner under the stairs. He piled them carefully in and around his bed and stamped them down to make a sort of platform.

The house looked instantly tidier, and McTavish was much more comfortable. So was Betty, who could now sit under the stairs with McTavish without having to push him over to make room for her on his bed. With all these nice sweaters and pillows, both Betty and McTavish could lie on their backs and stretch out their legs, a position everyone knows is excellent for thinking.

Betty and McTavish were delighted with Plan A. But not everyone in the family agreed.

Ava went on a rampage, claiming that her

best sweaters had disappeared from under the bed, which was where she usually kept them.

Ollie complained that there were no clean towels in the damp pile under the sink in the bathroom. Which was where he usually kept them.

Pa Peachey could not find two socks that matched in the huge heap of dirty clothes near the laundry basket. And if he did find two that matched, they smelled like old feet. Because nobody had washed them.

That's Ma Peachey's job, Pa Peachey thought, despite the fact that it no longer was.

The laundry pile was a particular triumph for McTavish. It included many soft and comfortable things to lie on and even one very fine Scottish cashmere cardigan.

McTavish was very fond of Scottish cashmere.

Now that he'd implemented Plan A, McTavish waited for the result.

He waited.

And he waited.

And he waited.

But nothing happened.

Nothing at all.

Not a single thing.

Not even one teensy, tiny thing.

Nothing.

And so he sighed and began to think again, and after some time, McTavish came up with Plan B.

9
PLAN B

Plan B consisted of chewing. McTavish chewed papers. He chewed boxes. He chewed gloves. But best of all, he chewed shoes. He focused most of his energy on chewing shoes.

Here's how he decided which shoes to chew.

He waited until everyone in the house had gone off to work or school, and then he scouted around looking for shoes that were not where they should be. Although chewing shoes is not a very nice habit for a dog, it must be said in his defense that he only chewed shoes that were out of place.

McTavish did not enter closets to find shoes. He did not touch shoes that were carefully lined up by a Peachey bedside (though to be fair, there were no such shoes). Had anyone left a tidy line of shoes by the front door, he would not have chewed them.

But all other shoes – or sneakers or slippers or boots – were fair game, particularly if one shoe was left lying at a great distance from its fellow shoe.

Let us pause here. It might be that you are beginning to think of McTavish as a bad and lazy dog. But you would be entirely wrong. Because chewing shoes is no job for a lazy dog. Chewing shoes is very hard work.

If you are not convinced that destroying an entire leather shoe with nothing but your teeth is hard work, perhaps you should try it sometime and see how it goes. Chances are you will begin to see what a difficult task McTavish had set out to accomplish.

In short, shoe-chewing is not a job for the faint of heart.

But McTavish was not a faint-hearted dog. He was a dog of great courage and purpose, and he was determined to make a success of Plan B.

On the third day of McTavish's shoe-chewing campaign, Alice called the Peachey family to see how they were doing with their new dog.

"How is dear, sweet, adorable McTavish?" Alice asked. "I can tell you that I had a great deal of trouble giving up that dog for adoption. I was very tempted to keep him for myself."

"*Dear* McTavish?" Pa Peachey snorted. "That dog is a monster."

"*Sweet* McTavish?" Ava Peachey exclaimed. "That dog is a rampant destroyer of shoes and an incorrigible collector of clothing."

"*Adorable* McTavish?" Ollie Peachey grumbled. "He will not look adorable when I kick him all the way to Mars for eating my favorite sneakers and dragging my best clothes into his bed."

"*Ohhhmmmm,*" hummed Ma Peachey.

Betty Peachey took the phone. "McTavish is doing very well, thank you, Alice. He is clever, affectionate, well organized, and intelligent. In addition, I have a strong feeling that McTavish is a dog with a plan."

Betty lowered her voice and crawled into the corner under the stairs for privacy. "And this family, Alice, is in desperate need of a plan."

At the other end of the phone, Alice sighed. "I fear you are correct, Betty. I suspected problems when I first met the Peachey family. But I have faith in McTavish. He has your best interests at heart, and if any dog can improve the muddled mess that is the Peachey family, it's McTavish."

"Yes," said Betty. "I am quite sure he is carrying out a plan as we speak, although I am not sure what it is."

"We must have faith."

"I have faith," said Betty. "He is a very good dog."

"Indeed he is," Alice said.

"Goodbye, Alice."

"Goodbye, Betty."

Betty emerged from the corner under the stairs to find the Peachey family standing in a semicircle, staring at her. Ollie held tight to McTavish, his fingers around the dog's tartan collar.

"We need a family meeting," Pa Peachey said.

"We really do," Ollie chimed in.

"A meeting," Ava added. "Now."

Pa Peachey opened the meeting.

"I am sorry to say it," he said, "but this dog, this so-called *McTavish*, is turning out to be nothing short of a disaster. He behaves like a hooligan, stealing our best clothes and dragging them into his lair."

"His 'lair'?" Betty said. "McTavish is not a dragon."

"He might as well be," Pa Peachey said.

"He has destroyed the very fabric of our family."

"He has destroyed the very fabric of my jeans," Ava said with a frown. McTavish had not, in fact, destroyed her jeans. He had merely added them to his comfy nest under the stairs, and did not offer to move when Ava came searching for them.

"If you had not left them on the floor by the laundry basket—" Betty began, but Pa Peachey interrupted.

"Ollie?" he said, pointing pointedly at his son. "Every member of the family must testify."

Betty rolled her eyes. "Is this the Supreme Court?" she asked. "Is this the War Crimes Commission?"

"Well," said Ollie, "McTavish has behaved badly. That is undeniable."

"I deny it entirely," Betty said. "We have behaved badly. We have left our clothes all over the floor, all over the kitchen, all over the stairs and the bathroom and every square inch of the house. No one can find anything in this house because of the chaos. It has spread to every room like some horrible creeping menace."

Ava glared at Betty. "The creeping menace is that dog of yours."

"McTavish does not creep," Betty said. "And he is not a menace."

Pa Peachey made a steeple of his fingers and tapped them together. Then he stood and cleared his throat. "We have heard from all parties," he said. "And it is clear that we have a bad and disruptive animal on our hands. I, however, have an idea."

The children all leaned forward. This

was the first time Pa Peachey had come up with an idea in as long as any of them could remember.

In the corner of the room, Ma Peachey practiced her looping cobra pose.

"I suggest," Pa Peachey said, "that from now on, we all put our clothes away in their proper places. I propose that we put laundry in the laundry basket. I propose that one person each week shall be assigned to sort, wash, and fold the laundry, and that each family member shall be responsible for returning his or her own clothes to his or her own room."

The children stared at him openmouthed.

"As for shoes," he said, "it would be a very good idea to take them off when you enter the house. And leave them in tidy pairs on the shoe rack by the front door." Pa Peachey said this in a calm tone of voice with no trace of anger. When he finished speaking, he sat down.

Ava and Ollie stared at their father in shock.

"I think that is a most wonderful and excellent idea," Betty said.

In the corner of the room, Ma Peachey executed a near-perfect looping cobra, which may or may not be what caused her to smile.

In his nest under the stairs, McTavish shut his eyes and sighed a contented sigh.

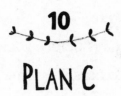

10
PLAN C

A hideous mess was no longer the first thing you saw upon entering the Peachey household. Shoes sat in tidy pairs by the front door. Clothes were neatly folded and put away in drawers. Car keys, homework, and sneakers no longer disappeared under piles of junk.

The Peachey home seemed to breathe more easily without its burden of chaos.

Family life improved. But not all their problems were solved.

In the old days before yoga, Ma Peachey had referred to herself – sometimes in jest – as the family alarm clock. She woke every morning at six thirty, put on the coffee, made breakfast, and only then shouted for everyone to wake up. Which they sometimes did and sometimes didn't.

Nowadays, she woke at six fifteen, prepared herself a cup of hot water and ginger to stimulate and cleanse the system, and practiced yoga for an hour and a half. Then she changed out of her yoga clothes, showered, applied lipstick, and made herself (herself *only*) a bowl of steel-cut oatmeal with antioxidant-rich berries. She left the house at eight fifteen on the dot.

Everyone else overslept.

Even when the alarm clock rang loud enough to wake the dead, most of the Peacheys slept on. Not Betty, who liked to use the early mornings to read a book. Not Ma Peachey, who liked to use early mornings to practice her crane pose. But everyone else.

Mornings for Ollie and Ava went like this.

Pa Peachey woke up late and shouted for Ollie and Ava to hurry. But they did not hurry. Ollie often had a bath with his headphones on, so he wouldn't hear Ava pounding on the bathroom door. Ava sometimes got distracted by Instagram. Everyone skipped breakfast while Pa Peachey slopped coffee onto the floor and sometimes down the front of his suit, which led to more shouting. It was not a pleasant start to the day.

After one particularly shouty Monday, on which all three children were late to school and Pa Peachey sloshed coffee everywhere, McTavish took the family schedule into his own four paws.

He referred to this privately as Plan C.

Dogs are not given nearly enough credit for their time-keeping abilities. If you doubt your dog's ability to tell time, here's a test. Take him (or her) out for a walk every day at exactly the same time. Do this for a week or two, and then one day, when walk time comes around, do not bother getting up from whatever you are doing to fetch the leash.

What do you suppose will happen?

If you own a dog, you know what will happen.

Your dog will come running with a hurt and puzzled look on her face. First, she will stare at you. If staring does not prove effective, she will begin to whine. If staring and whining do not prove effective, your dog will stand by the door, pacing back and forth like a caged beast. She might fetch her leash and drop it noisily onto the floor. Or put a paw in your lap with an insistent expression that says, *Walk. Now.*

Your dog will begin this show of impatience within a minute or two of when you normally walk her. Because dogs are very good at telling time. They do it without a clock or a watch or a phone.

Really, they do.

So what did McTavish do?

He set his own alarm clock. The one in his head.

At seven a.m. on the dot, he began barking to go out. He barked and barked, until one member of the family eventually got up, cursing and muttering, to let him out into the yard. That family member nearly always returned at once to bed, and thence to sleep.

McTavish waited just long enough for this to happen, and then began barking to come back in.

At this point, a muttering, cursing person – sometimes the same one, sometimes not – would get out of bed and let him back in, returning to bed while McTavish raced from room to room yapping and pawing and licking and wagging and generally making a complete nuisance of himself until every member of the muttering, cursing Peachey family was wide awake.

For a medium-size dog with very short legs, McTavish had a very impressive bark. Once he began to bark, it became impossible to stay in bed, so that eventually the Peacheys got up, still muttering and grumbling. Meanwhile, McTavish enjoyed an invigorating game of dodge the slipper, dodge the pillow, and dodge the books that were thrown at him in a spirit of deep resentment.

Only Betty got out of bed quietly and calmly, had a shower, got dressed, and went downstairs to prepare breakfast.

For the first few days, McTavish kept up the pressure until it was time to leave for school.

He growled when Ollie or Ava tried to go back to bed. He yapped and snapped when they lingered over breakfast. At precisely 7:55 a.m., he made a last circuit of the kitchen, where Ollie would be eating toast and Ava would be reading philosophy, where Pa Peachey would be fussing and dithering and Betty would be putting on her coat.

McTavish began howling at one minute to eight, so Betty knew it was time to fetch the leash and attach it to his collar. If any member of the family was not ready to leave the house by eight o'clock, he turned up the volume of his howl so that they had no choice but to leave the house. Or go crazy.

Ollie missed lying in bed until one minute to eight and arriving at school without breakfast, without his school books, and without most of his school uniform.

Ava occasionally used the early mornings to catch up on her reading of *Great Philosophical Riddles of the Western World*. She had no desire to get out of bed even when an insistent dog pulled her covers to the floor. She hissed threats at McTavish, such as, "I am going to call Animal Control. They will come and take you away."

"I didn't know we were getting an alarm clock," Pa Peachey said in a gloomy tone of voice. "I thought we were getting a dog."

"He *is* a dog," Betty said. "A dog who keeps time."

"He is so annoying," said Ollie, glaring at McTavish.

"I *like* lying in bed," Ava said. "Much more than I like going to school."

Not one single member of the family (except for Betty and Ma Peachey) appreciated the McTavish alarm clock.

"That dog," Pa Peachey said, "is an infernal nuisance, and I'm going to look into sending him back to the shelter."

But for the first time in months, all the Peacheys who needed to be out of the house at eight o'clock were out of the house at eight o'clock.

McTavish's people-training technique worked so well that after the first week he was able stop all his nagging, all his barking and howling. He had only to bark sharply once, at seven o'clock, and again at seven thirty to muster the Peacheys down for breakfast. At five minutes to eight, everyone was ready to go. Except for Ma Peachey, who could now practice her flying pigeon pose until 8:05, and then leave for work in a calm state of mind at eight fifteen.

Miraculously, mornings became almost civilized. And not one of the Peacheys was late to school or work ever again.

11

THE PEACHEYS
EAT PIZZA

It was a Saturday.

Ma Peachey had been practicing her dancing warrior all day, and it was nearly time for dinner, with no sign of anything to eat.

Betty looked thoughtful, and Ava broke off from her writing to shout (at no one in particular), "Is there anything for dinner, or are we all just going to starve?"

Ollie muttered that starvation was definitely on the menu.

At just that moment, Pa Peachey came in from the yard. He looked around, taking in the general tidiness of the house. For the first time in days, he smiled.

Ollie, Ava, and Betty greeted him.

"There's nothing in the fridge," Ava moaned.

"I've got an exam on Monday and I'm starving!" Ollie kicked the wall.

"We could order a pizza. Again," Betty said with a despondent air. Even pizza lost its appeal after the twelfth night in a row. "Maybe there's a flavor we haven't tried yet."

"There isn't," Ollie said, kicking the wall again.

The Peacheys ordered a pizza and sat around the table nibbling it listlessly. McTavish watched them eat. He was far too well mannered to beg at the table, but when

Ollie's unfinished slice found its way into McTavish's bowl, it was only polite of him to taste it.

McTavish licked the edge and walked away. Even he was sick of pizza.

Betty watched with a frown. McTavish hadn't eaten his dinner the night before. And now that she thought about it, he hadn't touched his breakfast this morning.

"Ava? Ollie? Has anyone been feeding McTavish on the sly?" asked Betty.

Ava and Ollie shook their heads.

Betty called Alice.

"Well," said Alice, sounding concerned, "I've never known McTavish to refuse food before. He's always been a good eater. But perhaps he's got a stomach bug. Try not feeding him at all tomorrow, but leave him

plenty of fresh water. Twenty-four hours without food should settle his stomach."

Betty didn't feed him the following day.

The day after, she tried again.

But McTavish just sniffed his food and went back to bed.

She called Alice again. "He hasn't eaten in three days, Alice. Should we take him to the vet?"

"Does he have any other symptoms? Loose bowels? Vomiting? Is he enjoying his walk? Does he seem cold? Or hot? Is he sleeping more than usual?"

Betty thought for a moment. "Not really, no, no, yes, no, no, no."

"Well," Alice said, "I suggest you try one more thing before taking him to the vet. It's the age-old cure for dogs who are off their food. Steamed chicken and rice."

"Steamed chicken and rice? That's all?" Betty said.

"That's all. It's simple and healthy, and if he's recovering from a bug, it won't upset him. If he eats the chicken and rice, then the next day you can add some lightly steamed vegetables. Nothing too strong – peas, maybe, a little spinach or some sweet potato."

Betty put down the phone, took some money out of her piggy bank, put on her coat, and went out to the store. She bought some very nice plump chicken breasts and a package of rice, brought it home, followed the instructions on the rice, and looked up a recipe for poached chicken breasts on the internet.

After ten minutes, Ollie and Ava gravitated to the kitchen like iron filings drawn to a magnet.

"What's that amazing smell?" Ollie asked.

Ava pulled the lid off the pan with the lightly poached chicken breasts in it, closed her eyes, and sniffed.

"Mmm," she said. "Real food at last!"

Betty took the lid from Ava's hand and replaced it. "It's for McTavish," she said. "He's not well, and I'm making him a special dinner."

Pa Peachey arrived home from work at just that moment.

"What's that delicious smell?" he called from the hall. "Don't tell me we're not having pizza tonight? That *is* good news!"

Betty informed him that the meal was for McTavish.

For a miserable moment the entire family stood in the kitchen smelling the delicious smell of poached chicken and rice.

Then Ollie sighed, picked up the phone, and ordered pizza. Again.

"So it has come to this," Pa Peachey sighed. "The animal eats like royalty while we scrabble about in the trash heap for scraps like vermin. McTavish is king, and we? We are nothing but rats."

Everyone ignored him.

Betty checked the chicken for doneness, prodded the rice with a fork, chopped the food into bite-size pieces, poured some of the stock into the bowl, allowed it to cool, and placed it on the floor.

"McTavish," she called softly. "Come and have something to eat."

It is worth noting that dogs have a sense of smell at least a thousand times better than humans'. At Betty's call, McTavish stood up, approached his bowl, sniffed it, took a small bite, chewed for a moment, and then downed the rest of the meal in a flash.

"Good boy, McTavish!" Betty said, relieved.

"Good boy? Good boy?" Pa Peachey was outraged. "Who wouldn't be a good boy, eating tender chicken breasts while the rest of us gnaw crusts with our gruel?"

No one spoke a word during their usual dinner of takeout pizza, except for Pa Peachey, who occasionally muttered something about rats.

The next day, Betty poached more chicken. Only this time, she added peas, a little spinach, and some sweet potato. Once again, the Peacheys huddled around the kitchen, craning their necks and sniffing the delicious aroma of poached chicken, rice, and fresh vegetables.

McTavish gulped down his whole dinner, just as he'd done the night before. He even licked the bowl afterward, in case he might have missed something. The entire Peachey family sighed when he finished. They were quiet, each thinking how nice it would be to have a lovely chicken dinner with vegetables prepared at home in their very own kitchen.

If only Ma Peachey would stop practicing her cow-face pose, her star pose, and her lizard lunge, and return to cooking.

For a long moment, nobody spoke. At last, Betty broke the silence.

"What if . . ." she began.

Everyone leaned forward, wondering what on earth she would say next.

"What if," she went on, "we were to borrow some of McTavish's food and cook a special dinner tonight?"

"Dog food?" gasped Pa Peachey. "Oh, that is rich. It's not enough that we're reduced to sifting through the trash for crumbs and crusts, for leftovers and leavings, for scrapings and scraps. Now we're reduced to eating dog food." He clapped a hand to his forehead. "Thank goodness my sainted parents didn't live to see this day."

"Granny and Granddad are alive and well," Betty said with a stern look. "And the food McTavish has been eating is not dog food. It is food. Good food. It is much nicer than the food we've been eating every night. It is healthy and delicious. And although it is more expensive than dog food, it is, in fact . . ." She pulled out a notebook and pencil, scribbled some sums, and then looked up. "It is definitely cheaper than pizza."

The Peacheys gasped as one. "Cheaper than pizza?"

"And better," said Betty. "Healthier and more delicious."

"But what about Ma Peachey?" Ollie asked. "Isn't she supposed to cook our dinner?"

"Ma Peachey has decided to seek inner peace in India," Betty said. "And to cook no more. So perhaps we should just get on with cooking for ourselves, rather than night after night eating food we don't like."

The Peacheys all stared at Betty as if she had just discovered a cure for the common cold.

"Really?" said Ava. "Us *cook*? Is that even possible?"

"Us?" said Ollie. "Us *cook*? Is that even legal?"

"Yes," said Betty. "I believe it is possible. And legal."

"Well, what are we waiting for?" Ollie was already sprinting to the fridge.

That night, the Peacheys all helped with the cooking. They pan-fried chicken breasts in lemon juice and olive oil and served them on a bed of steamed spinach and rice, with a side of roasted sweet potato sprinkled with pumpkin seeds. It was the most delicious meal any of them could remember eating in as long as any of them could remember.

From his post under the stairs, McTavish observed the goings-on through half-closed eyes. If you hadn't known he was a dog, you might have thought that the expression on his face was a teensy bit smug.

12

THE PEACHEYS
PITCH IN

For the next ten days, the Peacheys all
pitched in to do the shopping, the cooking,
and the cleaning up.

They discovered that cooking is not
difficult. It is simpler than learning to play
professional billiards or becoming a ballerina
or flying a jumbo jet. Ollie, in particular, was
stunned at how easy it was to follow a recipe.

"Hey, this is a lot easier than studying

for a chemistry exam," he said with an air of astonishment. "And it's even easier now than it was last week."

Ava was chopping onions, wearing an old diving mask they had bought for a beach vacation many years ago.

"I kind of like chopping," she said. "It's a whole lot less difficult than reading French philosophy."

Betty sat by the stove, stirring and tasting.

When the three Peachey children worked together, they could produce an excellent, healthy meal in not much more than half an hour.

They cooked sausages and mashed potatoes with steamed green beans in no time at all. It was so delicious, Ava felt like fainting.

They made spaghetti Bolognese in less

time than it took to study a takeout menu and decide what to eat.

They made vegetable soup and roasted chicken.

They made pumpkin curry and rice.

They attempted to outdo one another with the ease and deliciousness of their recipes.

Each night Pa Peachey came home in a better mood than he had the night before. The meals that greeted him were tasty and tempting. They were beautifully prepared and presented.

"What's this?" Pa Peachey demanded one night, about a meal so beautiful and tempting, he might have put it on his Facebook page. If he'd had one.

"It is fish pie," said Betty. "I made the crust, which is far simpler than it looks. Then

I added some fish, carrots, and frozen peas, plus a simple sauce, and *voilà!*" She held out the golden steaming pie so the whole family could say, "*Ooh!*"

The whole family said, "*Ooh!*"

Even Ma Peachey looked up from her flying dolphin pose to say, "*Ooh!*"

Betty served up her fish pie and smiled modestly as every member of the family clapped her on the back and told her that she was an amazing cook for a not-quite-nine-year-old, or even for an actual person, and that her fish pie tasted even better than it looked.

Only Ollie lowered the tone by saying that he wished they had made chocolate cake for dessert.

"Maybe tomorrow," Betty said. And, still smiling, she scraped the leftovers (though there weren't many) into McTavish's bowl. McTavish tasted the fish pie and turned to Betty.

"*Ooh!*" he woofed.

Plan C, McTavish thought, had been an excellent plan. This was the best fish pie he'd ever eaten. Possibly the best fish pie of all time.

He licked his chops and toddled back to bed, feeling very satisfied with his life. And very proud of his Peacheys.

13

A MOST IMPRESSIVE DOG

The day after the fish pie triumph, Ma Peachey woke up very early. She got out of bed, showered, dressed, and padded down to the kitchen.

"Hello, McTavish," she said to McTavish.

McTavish heaved himself out of a peaceful slumber to greet her, stretching into a textbook example of the downward dog pose.

Ma Peachey bent down and gazed into

his eyes. "You don't think I've noticed," she whispered. "But I have. You are quite an impressive dog, and I have a great deal to thank you for."

McTavish smiled, in the way that dogs smile, with a soft little woof and a squirmy sort of wriggle.

Ma Peachey kissed McTavish on the top of the head and straightened up. But she didn't unroll her yoga mat. She didn't perform her salutation to the sun pose. She didn't click Buy on the flights to India in her online shopping basket.

Instead, she went to the kitchen and began to take out the ingredients for chocolate cake.

Ma Peachey hummed as she beat the sugar and butter. She whistled as she folded in eggs, flour, baking powder, and melted

chocolate. An hour later, she positively broke into song as she traced a large 9 on the finished cake along with the words *Happy Birthday, Betty.*

McTavish went back to bed with a contented sigh. *Humans make excellent pets,* he thought. When you took on a rescue family, it often took some weeks for them to settle, but he was glad he'd decided to adopt the Peacheys.

As with most humans, all they'd needed was training, combined with common sense and discipline. Despite their early lack of promise, McTavish felt certain that the Peacheys would turn out fine. With a little more work and a consistent routine, they would turn out to be a most satisfactory family after all.